Archie

Sutherland

For Nicola (who continues to adapt well to the ways of Earth).
Thanks for everything - S.B.

A TEMPLAR BOOK

First published in the UK in hardback in 2002 by Templar Publishing
This audio edition published in 2005 by Templar Publishing,
an imprint of The Templar company plc,
Pippbrook Mill, London Road, Dorking, Surrey, RH4 1JE, UK
www.templarco.co.uk

Copyright © 2002 by Simon Bartram

The illustrations for this book were painted in acrylics on paper.

Limited audio edition, third impression

ISBN-13: 978-1-84011-369-3

Designed by Mike Jolley
Edited by Marcus Sedgwick

Printed in Hong Kong

Man on the Moon

(a day in the life of Bob)

Simon Bartram

templar publishing

This is **Bob**. Perhaps you've heard people talk of him. You may know him better as the **Man on the Moon**.

This is where Bob lives. Every morning he rises at six o'clock. He has a cup of tea and two eggs for breakfast, before leaving for the rocket launch-pad. On the way he stops to buy a newspaper and some chocolate toffees.

He's on his way to work...

...on the MOON!

By eight o'clock Bob arrives at the launch-pad, changes into his special Man on the Moon suit and boards his fantastic rocket ship.

He must make sure he leaves by a quarter to nine, otherwise he wouldn't make it to the Moon by nine.

On the way he reads the newspaper and does the crossword.

Bob starts work. His job as Man on the Moon is very important. He has to keep the Moon clean and tidy. Quite often astronauts drop sweet packets and cans.

Some people say that aliens are responsible for much of the rubbish, but Bob knows that's not true. There's no such thing as aliens...

By twelve-thirty it's time to eat.

Bob goes to his rocket ship to fetch his lunch
box. This usually contains two sandwiches
(either cheese or peanut butter), an apple
and some chocolate covered nuts.

Sometimes he meets his friends for a picnic.
His two best friends are Billy, the Man on Mars,
and Sam, the Man on Saturn. They talk about
the stars, and tell jokes.

After lunch, tourist spaceships start arriving
from Earth.
It is part of Bob's job to entertain them,
and give them something to photograph,

so he does somersaults, handstands and especially high moon jumps. Sometimes he performs for as long as two hours and is left quite out of puff.

Occasionally, the tourists' spaceships will land on the Moon. When they do, Bob gives them a guided tour, and a speech. He tells them lots of facts, such as how many craters the Moon has, or how long it takes to walk around it on stilts.

Sometimes people ask him about aliens, and Bob explains patiently that there aren't any.

Afterwards, Bob opens a small souvenir stand, selling postcards, pencils, mugs and small plastic Moon models.

By four-thirty all visitors must leave the Moon. Bob looks around to see that everyone has left. He checks inside any big craters in case anyone has fallen in - but there's **never** anyone there.

The working day is nearly over - it is time to check everything is in order before leaving for the night. Bob packs away his equipment and any unsold souvenirs into his rocket.

He switches on the Moon's nightlight before jetting off towards Earth.

By this time he is very tired, but he still has to keep his wits about him while flying the rocket.

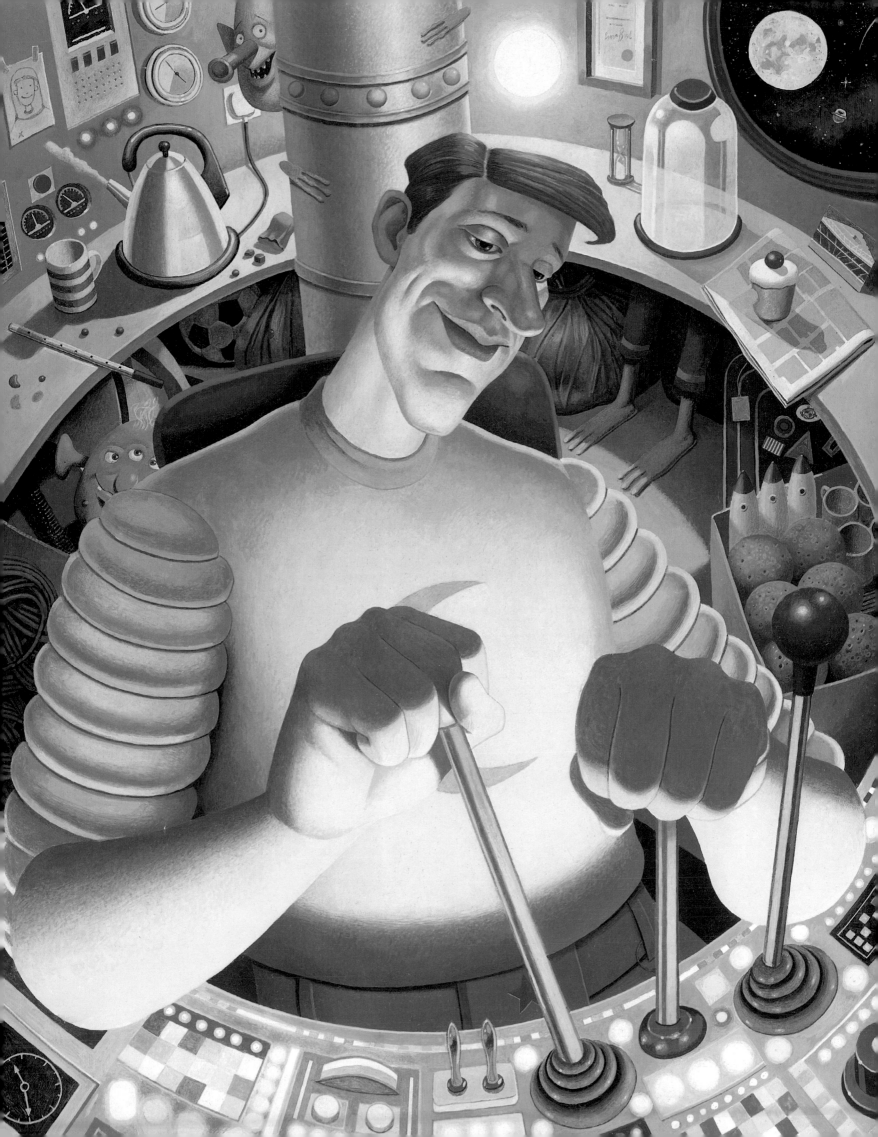

As he reaches Earth it's about five o'clock.

The rush hour is in full swing with everyone
leaving work and going home. Just like Bob.

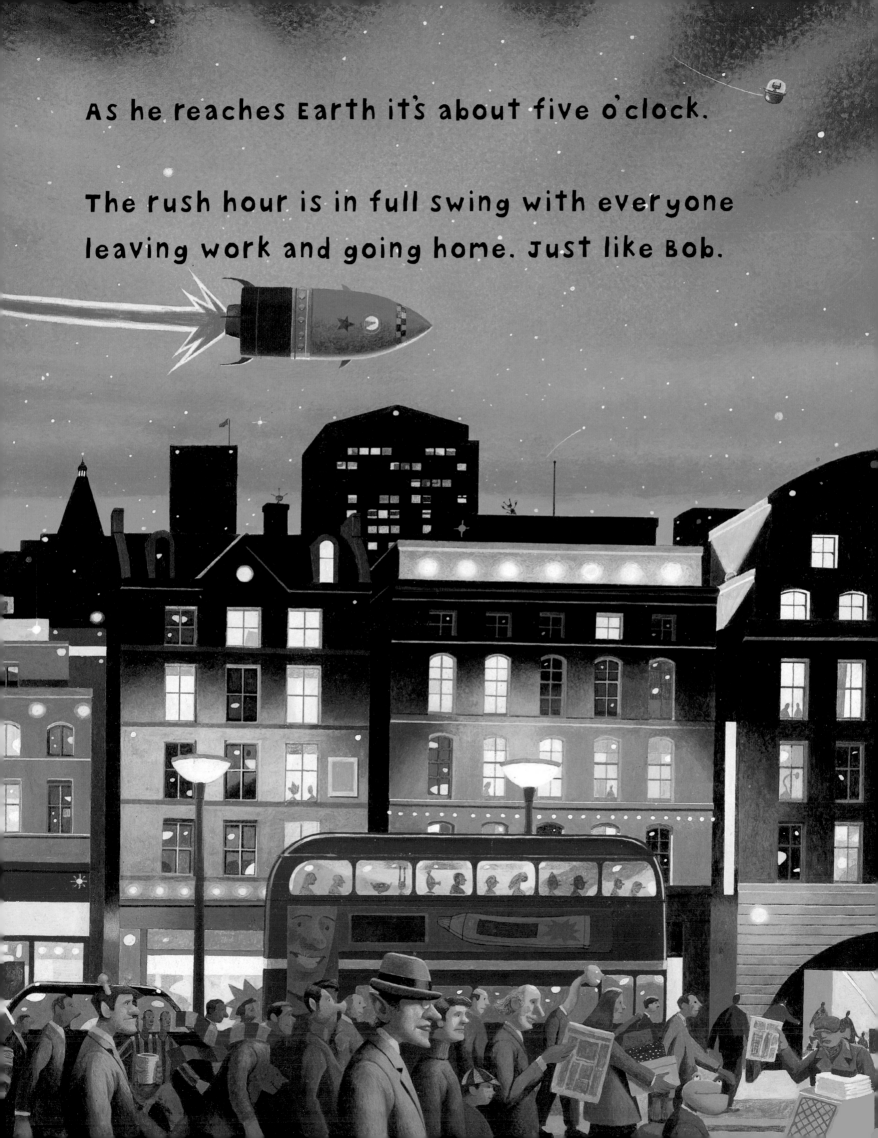

At home Bob is just like anyone else. First he has a long bath. Moon-work can make you very grubby as sometimes the dust can get inside your suit.

Then he goes to bed with a mug of cocoa. He sleeps soundly, bathed in moonbeams, very happy to be the Man on the Moon.

And aliens...?

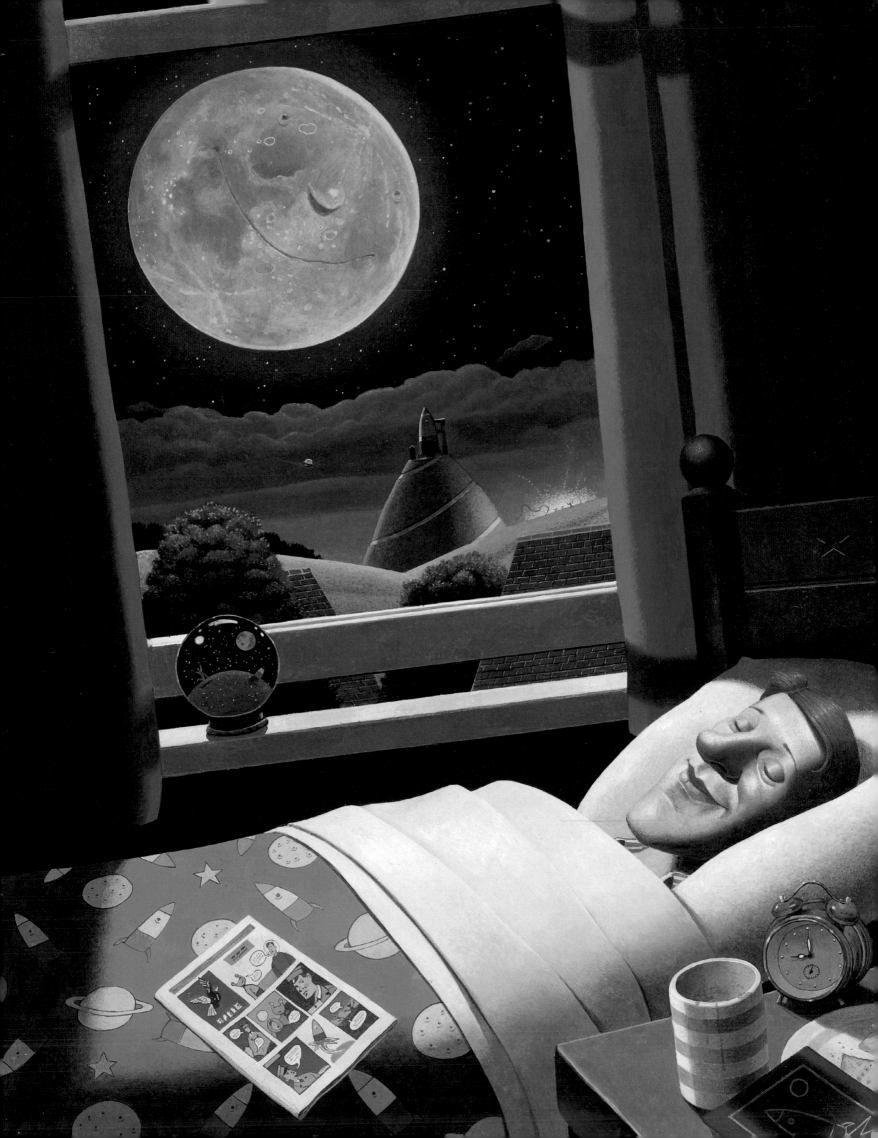

...well, Bob **would** know if there were any...

wouldn't he?